# A LINE OF DRIFTWOOD

―――――――

## THE ADA BLACKJACK STORY

Requests for permissions to make
copies of any part of the work should
be sent to:
Turtle Point Press, 208 Java Street,
Fifth Floor, Brooklyn, NY, 11222
info@turtlepointpress.com

Library of Congress Catalogue-in-
Publication Data

Names: Glancy, Diane, author.
Title: A line of driftwood : the Ada
Blackjack story / Diane Glancy.
Other titles: Ada Blackjack story
Identifiers: LCCN 2021025604 | ISBN
9781933527215 (trade paperback)
Subjects: LCSH: Blackjack, Ada,
1898-1983--Poetry. | Blackjack, Ada,
   1898-1983--Diaries. | Inupiat women--
Poetry. | Wrangel Island
   (Russia)--Poetry. | LCGFT:
Biographical poetry.
Classification: LCC PS3557.L294 L56
2021 | DDC 811/.54 [B]--dc23
LC record available at https://lccn.loc.
gov/2021025604

Book design by Zab Hobart

ISBN: 978-1-933527-21-5

Printed in the United States of
America

First Edition

Ada Blackjack [1898-1983], Inupiat, the only survivor of a 1921-23 expedition to Wrangel Island in the Arctic Ocean.

———————

Ada Blackjack went as a seamstress with four explorers to Wrangel Island in the Arctic Ocean in September 1921. After rations ran out, and the supply ship did not arrive because of ice, the team was unable to kill enough game on the island to survive. Three of the men tried to cross 200 miles of the frozen sea to Siberia for help. They were never seen again. The fourth explorer was too ill to travel because of scurvy. When he died, Ada kept his frozen body in his deerskin sleeping bag. She was alone two months before the rescue ship arrived in August 1923. Ada is buried in Anchorage. She died at 85.

———————

I held Ada's diary in the Rauner Collections at Dartmouth College. She wrote of daily activities, but underneath was the voice of her journey along the actual events.

# PROLOGUE

# PART ONE
The Voice of Her Journey

# PART TWO
Ada's Writings and Diary

# PART THREE
Epilogue

# Appendix

# A LINE OF DRIFTWOOD

---

## THE ADA BLACKJACK STORY

*Diane Glancy*

TURTLE POINT PRESS

*BROOKLYN, NEW YORK*

# SCAR

———

I HAVE A SCAR that cuts my eyebrow in half. A short, half-worm mark. A sliver now. I received it as a child. I thank the Holy Father, the God of falls, that glass did not cut my eye. I jumped up in a chair that fell backwards into a glass-doored bookcase beside the fireplace. I have a larger scar in my scalp. I was running. Maybe seeking to leap from earth.

No, that's not what happened. What happened was that I was captive on an island with polar bears. Maybe it was a thought trying to get in my head. Maybe I was dealing with something not yet understood. A realization I could not handle. I was fleeing to the shore across the room where a chair, the rescue boat, waited. I jumped for the boat to escape the polar bear. My scar something like a small oar-handle.

But even that might not be true. The door I fell into was ice, not glass. It was Eskimos I was running from with their whale harpoons and seal spears. What I didn't know was that the Eskimos were in myself. They were myself. The cold and the ice also were in myself. All those spikes were not mother, father, brother, but myself.

But even that was not true. What might be more true is this. I was in the house. I was bored. What could I do? Maybe my mother chased me like a polar bear. Maybe I was clawed after playing roughly with my younger brother. The scar is like a claw mark in my eye-brow. There was nothing to do in the house. I was there, but not wanted there. And not wanting to be there. But having no place else to go. A Wrangel Island of sorts. It's why I knew Ada Blackjack's voice. I was the boat she ran toward.

Notes to myself to keep going—
It is Arctic exploration from a woman's point-of-view.
It is written for the 100th anniversary of the expedition.
It is a positive report of residential school attendance.

When Ada's mother could not care for her there was a place Ada could go. The Methodist Mission taught Ada to write. It gave her an intersection of time and place that would carry her to the boat that came to rescue her from Wrangel Island. It taught her to believe when there was nothing to hold onto.

# PART ONE

---

THE VOICE OF HER JOURNEY

## ADA BLACKJACK

---

1.

They ate me like horsemeat.
Yet I survived.

A horse is not an Arctic animal.
Neither were they.

I was marooned on an island with four explorers—
Allan Crawford, Lorne Knight, Fred Maurer, Milton Galle.

I went to a shaman before we left Nome.
There was death and danger for the expedition.

We departed on a boat September 10th, 1921
and arrived at Wrangel Island in the Arctic Ocean September 16th.
The men raised a flag and claimed the island for Great Britain.
We unloaded supplies on the black gravel shore.
It looked large to me, but the men said it was small.
I thought at first I would turn back, but I was a seamstress
who spoke English.

I learned to write in the Methodist Mission.
What is written is what lasts—

The letters of the alphabet are an elk herd—
the branching of antlers.
The curve of belly.
The knot of hooves.
The straight lines of legs for other letters.

The numbers I learned to write were birds.

I was not alone on the island.
The ice was with me.
The cold was with me.
The expedition cat, Victoria, was with me.

The sled dogs were caged during travel on the ship.
I think Victoria taunted them.
They glared at her when she was outside.
But they were chained and could not chase her.
She seemed to know how far they could leap.

There were no trees on Wrangel Island.
But there were piles of driftwood on the shore.
The men hauled driftwood to make a wood pile for winter.

When it snowed, they made a frame for the snow-house
and put the snow blocks in.
We were living in a tent and it was cold.

I sewed snow shirts for the men.
We brought reindeer-skin parkas and all I had to do
was fasten the shirts to the parkas.

I was sorry I came on the expedition.
I felt stranded with the men when the boat left us on the island.

The missionaries said I would not be alone.
I had Jesus.
But I had married Jack Blackjack and he deserted me.

Now I loved Allen Crawford.
I followed him around the camp.
The men teased him.
They laughed.
I was an outcast.
I had crying spells.
I missed my son, Bennett, and my sister.

I wanted to be with Crawford.
I thought he would marry me.
The men were together in a group.
I was by myself.

The men made a camp for me farther away from Crawford.
I walked to his tent.
He would not let me in.

Minus forty degrees—
For days we were confined to our tents.
Victoria, the cat, crept around the camp.
At night she found a sleeping bag to crawl inside.

I like writing words on paper.
It is similar to sewing.
Each letter I write is a stitch.
I kept a journal with my Eversharp pencil.

Some days I sewed.
Some days I wrote in my journal.

Sometimes I could not tell the difference between sewing and writing.

The Polar Lights prowled like polar bears.
The men watched the lights.
What good were they?
We could not hunt the lights.
We could not eat them.

We passed into days of darkness when everything was the same.
I didn't know if it was night or day.
Or what day or night it was.

I held up my hand asking the Polar Lights to take me with them.

Desperation slipped into sleep with me.

I repaired parkas.
I repaired boots.
In the distance, the driftwood looked like stitches someone had taken in the snow.

I was afraid of Lorne Knight.
He grumbled like a walrus.
Whenever I came near their camp, he bundled me up,
strapped me to the sled, and took me back to my tent.
I screamed at him.

What do you do, Ada— he asked— but eat our food?

The next morning, I walked to Crawford's tent again.
I heard the men playing cards.

I walked back to my camp.
I refused to repair another pair of boots.

When I came back to their camp,
Lorne Knight tied me to the flagpole until I said I would work.
He left me tied to the pole a long time.
I started howling and he let me go and I returned to my tent.

Mr. Knight told me to make mittens and skin-socks
and scrape deerskin while he trapped.
But I did nothing.

He said if I didn't work, I wouldn't eat.

Mr. Knight got his Bible and read to me.
It reminded me of the mission school.

The men didn't want me.
I could die and they would be relieved.
I would go back to Nome on the first supply ship that came.
Let them sew their own clothes.

I stopped following Crawford.
I was useless as a horse.

I learned to think of myself as others saw me.
It was my first lesson on Wrangel Island.

2.

The men had trouble hunting and trapping.

I had been raised in the mission school.
I didn't know what to do, either.

When the men knew the rations would not last—
when they could not catch enough game to feed us—
when they knew the ship would not return before winter
with more supplies— they were mean.

Two of my sons with Jack Blackjack died.
The third, Bennett, had tuberculosis.
The men knew my husband left me.
They knew the two boys died.
I was incompetent, they said.
I was an Eskimo that did not know how to survive in the cold.

The men stayed up late.
I heard them from my tent.
Sound carries across the ice.
They did not know what to do.

One of the sled dogs died.
The men had to feed them cornmeal when supplies were low.
The men built a doghouse.
They had to have shelter from the fierce winds and cold.

A polar bear crept near the camp.
It thinks no one knows it is there.
It should be aware of how it is seen.
Victoria, the cat, stiffens.

I read the list of what the men brought—
5000 pounds groceries
guns
ammunition
traps
harpoons
fish nets
fishhooks
thermometers
flashlights
batteries
lanterns
stoves
cooking gear
shovels
ice picks and other hardware
canvas
camera
field glasses
books

Milton Galle brought his typewriter that no one else could use.

Each man was given 12 pair socks, 11 pair trousers, skin
mitts, blanket mitts, skin shirts, belts, undershirts, one pair
drawers and one suit of underwear, water boots, canvas boots,
handkerchiefs, towels.

I would make the rest of the clothing they needed—
Ada Blackjack, the seamstress.

Some of the supplies were not with the others.
The potatoes rotted.

The prunes had maggots.
The sled dogs were thin.

Sometimes I heard Victoria licking the seal-oil cans
at the trash heap.

I read my own list of supplies—
11 towels
3 handkerchiefs
1 bed
I was given clothing for the journey.
I was given money to buy sinew, linen thread, needles, and
thimbles.
I was given a journal in which to write.
I was given an Eversharp pencil.
I had not held a pencil since I was at the Methodist Mission.
$50 a month would be deposited in the bank in Nome for me.

I remembered the shaman's words—
I should beware of knives and fire—
but the men needed a seamstress who could speak English.

We left Nome on the Silver Wave.
We stopped at East Cape, Siberia, to get more sinew and white
sealskin.
We also bought a small Eskimo skin boat— an umiak.
After we left East Cape, we ran into a storm.
We tossed for two days.
The umiak was blown overboard.
The engine of the Silver Wave broke down,
and we had to lay over a half-day and night
until the men got it working again.

I should have stayed on the boat when we arrived at Wrangel
Island.

At first, we had a single tent.
The men slept in the larger part of the tent.
I slept in the smaller part that also was the kitchen.

There were mountains in the distance.
Streams. Lichen. Moss. Wildflowers.

The men wrote in their journals.
Milton Galle typed what he wrote.
His typing sounded like cards shuffling.
The men made furniture. Repaired equipment. Hunted.
And hunted.

I sewed for the men. Repaired gloves and boots.
I made hoods for their parkas.

I was shut away on the island.
I wanted Bennett, my young son, and my sister.
I cried and could not stop.
I tried to think about something else.
But Bennett and my sister stayed in my head.
I cried until I irritated the men.

The men moved the camp so they didn't have to haul
the driftwood so far.
Eventually, the men made three camps.
Two men in one tent. Two men in another.
Myself in the third. Farthest away in a tent.
As far as possible from Crawford.

The men had to keep moving.
The sameness would turn them against one another.

The men began to realize the lack of game on the island.
They killed a fox. A seal. A bear.

The wind trotted over the island. The cold. The cold.

I drank a bottle of liniment one day.
I walked out of my tent across the snow.
I didn't know where I was going.
Maybe I would find a ship in the bay— beyond the ice.
Yes, a ship would be there.
If I kept walking.
I walked until I felt heavy with the cold.
I fell to my knees.
I rested on the snow and let myself fall into sleep.

I heard something— I opened my eyes.
Was it a polar bear?
The spirits that haunted the dying?
I didn't want to go to the next life.
No, it was the men approaching.
No— I screamed.
I kicked them away.

They left me alone until I came back to myself.

3.

Supplies were low.
Sometimes the ocean cleared so a boat could come in.
If the ice went out, it came in again.
We knew a boat would not come before the next winter.
We would not have enough to eat.
I heard fear in their voices again.

The men didn't talk to me. They talked to each other.
Sometimes they watched me. They liked to watch me sew.
That is how it is done, they must be thinking.
But explorers knew how to sew.
I saw them sew when I was stewing.

I'm not sure what they knew. Other than they were desperate.

Maybe they should go for help— I listened to Allan Crawford's
words.
They could make it to Siberia for help.

There was still in me what longed for another.

4.

All that fall the men hunted and came back with little.

I put the few hides on stretchers. Seal skin. Fox skin.

I found a calendar book for 1922.
I marked off the days. Summer was gone.
The clouds shut the sun in their little icehouse.

I saw a raven cross the sky.
Its outstretched wings made a slice into the horizon.

One day, I pecked once on Galle's typewriter
and did not do it again.

Milton Galle's typing sounded like a raven squawking—
waughk
w aughk
w a ughk
w a u ghk
w a u g hk
w a u g h k
I listened to the letters separate from their words.

Victoria, the cat, went outside when Galle typed.

By afternoon, there was wind and blowing snow.

I listened to the men talk.
Fred Maurer had been on Wrangel Island before.
He was part of the Vilhjalmur Stefansson 1913 Canadian Arctic
Exploration.

Their ship, the *Karluk*, caught in the ice and carried the crew
north.
Stefansson left the ship and walked south across the ice.
He deserted the ship, Maurer said.
When the *Karluk* sank, the crew walked 100 miles
on the ice to Wrangel Island. Lorne Knight was on another ship,
*The Polar Bear.*
When he saw Stefansson walking across the ice, they picked
him up.
Meanwhile, many of Stefansson's crew died on Wrangel Island.
Stefansson also had organized this second voyage to Wrangel
Island.
Deserted by Stefansson once again, Knight agreed with Maurer.

We spent days in our tents.
Winter lasted into the next summer.

Fierce winds. Cold temperatures.

We hauled driftwood. We rationed food.

We looked into the bay with the field glasses.
We knew a boat would arrive.

5.

A supply boat did not arrive.
If only we could eat driftwood.

We looked out into the bay. We saw the ice.
A boat would be crushed as the Karluk had— Maurer said.

We tried to hide our disappointment.

The geese came. The geese went.
Everything that could move seemed to migrate away
from Wrangel Island except the ice.

August was the only month without snow.
I gathered wildflowers.
I looked at their patterns thinking how I could sew them
on my mukluks, reindeer parka, and gloves.

The men shot a walrus.
It took more effort to cut and haul the parts of it back to camp
than the men could make.

They were starving.

I cooked for them.
They complained of the sameness of every meal.
I found roots.
I boiled them.
I fried them.
I cooked with cocoa.

Allan Crawford drew maps.

Milton Galle had an abscessed tooth.

The men made excursions.
Mr. Knight came back nearly frozen when he fell into a stream.
His legs hurt. He was ill. He was irritable.
I thought he might have scurvy.

The men killed a few seals.
I told Knight to eat as much blubber as he could.

I cooked until we could hardly eat for the plainness.

6.

I am not alone.
I have writing.
I have the Polar Lights.
They move across the sky as though they were writing.

For Christmas, we had salted seal meat
and hard bread and tea for dinner.

January 8th, 1923, Lorne Knight and Allan Crawford left for
Siberia to look for help.
Around January 21st they came back because Mr. Knight
was sick.

They talked about three of the men taking the trip.
It would be easier for three men to make a snow house when
they camped.

About January 28th Allan Crawford, Fred Maurer and Milton
Galle left for Siberia.
They left with the five dogs and a large sled of supplies.
They left me with Lorne Knight who was sick with scurvy.
No one ever saw them again.

I dreamed of sled dogs eaten.
The frozen bodies of the men piled on each other like
driftwood on the shore.

Other times the driftwood looked like letters of the alphabet.

At first Knight seemed to be all right.
He chopped a little wood, but fainted.

I told him I would chop wood and bring in snow for water.
I was used to it, I said.
He knew I was not, but he didn't say anything.

The men took some instruments but left some for Mr. Knight.
I practiced shooting empty cans.
I used the gun and knife.
I can shoot like them.
Nearly.
The white fox, polar bear, seal, birds belong to the Arctic.
The four men did not.

How much like a gun were words.

## 7.

Fred Maurer gave Mr. Knight the map of his trap lines before
they left.
When I tried to find the trap lines, I only could find six or
seven traps.

Three or four days later, I found the rest, but there was no fox
in any of them.

I set trap lines for a month and never caught a fox.

I was afraid of meeting a polar bear.
I kept turning around to see if one was in sight.
If there had of been one, I would have fainted.
I only had a snow knife with me and didn't know what to do to
defend myself.
I never carried a rifle when I went out on the trap lines.

I went every day.
I had to get something for Mr. Knight to eat.
He was still sick and we had nothing in the tent.

I became weak from tramping around and thought I would
give up, but one day I noticed some fox tracks around one of
the traps.
I dug the trap out of the snow.
In setting up the fox traps, you bait them, and then cover
them with a little snow.
But I guess I covered them too much and that was the reason I
didn't get any fox.
Then I baited the trap again, and just left it on top of the snow,
and didn't cover it at all.

The next morning I got up, and looked out, and saw a fox.
I didn't know if it was in the trap or not, but I dressed and
went out— and there was a white fox in the trap— that was the
first fox I had caught!— February 23rd 1923.

After that I caught more.
I would take a stick and hit them on the head, stunning them.
Then I would bend their heads back until I broke the neck.

Later in the spring, around April, the fox got very scarce, and I
couldn't trap any more at all.

Around May, I think, I took a walk across the ice
toward the small islands in the harbor, and a seagull flew over
my head.
I had brought a shot gun with me this time, one that belonged
to Mr. Knight, and I shot at it with my gun and killed it.
I took it home and made some broth for Mr. Knight for he
could eat very little.

8.

I am not alone on the island.
Sometimes I feel my father with me.
I dreamed of him when he was sick.
He ate bad meat.
I was 8 years old.
My sister and I dressed him in his pants and parka—
wrapped him in skins and put him on the sled.
We hitched the dogs and started to Nome 30 miles from
Spruce Creek.
He died on the way.

My mother sent me to Nome, where I learned to write and sew
and read the Bible in the Methodist Mission.

I married Jack Blackjack.
Two children died.
After the third child, Bennett, was born, Blackjack abandoned
me.

I returned to my mother in Nome.
I took my son, Bennett, to an orphanage.
He has tuberculosis.
I couldn't care for him.
I worked in Nome, but couldn't earn enough to support us.

If I uttered a word, Mr. Knight heard it.
He uttered back-
No wonder my two children died.
No wonder my husband was mean to me.
No wonder my third child is sick in an orphanage.

All bitterness came from him.
The disgruntled one.
The old walrus who couldn't wallow across the rock.

I held the bedpan for Mr. Knight.
I pushed it in his deerskin sleeping bag.
Sometimes I think he did not wait for it to get to where it
should go.
He was dying.
He was letting go.
He did not want to.

He was immoveable.
He was bleeding out the nose.
In February, when he first got sick,
he gave me his Bible that had belonged to his grandfather.

If a ship came, it could not bring him back.
His journey was not to Nome.
Not to his own country.
But to what death was.
Even he knew.
His anger was that he didn't want to go where he was going.

The men were going to claim Wrangel Island.
But the land claimed them.
That was their discovery.
It was another lesson on Wrangel Island.

9.

Mr. Knight is suffering.
He cannot get up from his deerskin sleeping bag.

Why don't I say something, he says when he can speak.
I don't have anything to say, I say to him.
He throws a book at me.

I listen to him breathe.
Sometimes at night, I listen when his breath nearly stops.
Then he breathes again.

There are blue splotches on his legs.
Some of his teeth fall out.
I would find one behind his ear.
Stuck in his hair.

I make him a pillow from a sack of Victoria's cat meal,
and put it under his back when he says it hurts.

I remembered the shaman's words.
There was death ahead for the expedition.

Once Mr. Knight tied to me to the flagpole.
Now he was tied to his bed.

10.

My face is swollen.
My eye nearly closed.
My throat is sore this morning.
Mr. Knight wants me to go to the trap lines, but I don't want
to go.

When my eye is better, my stomach hurts.
I haven't been out for days.

Eventually I have to get snow to melt for water.

I opened a can of biscuits and chopped wood.

I found a frozen fox in one of the traps.
It was nothing but skin and bones.

I opened a can of oil.

Two days later, I found a fox with good meat.

I read the Bible.

When the weather cleared, I walked to an island for some
roots.
I shot a bird and saw a polar bear.

Mr. Knight can hardly talk.

I went to a little island and found three seagull eggs.
I cooked them for lunch and had a picnic all to myself.

11.

I did not know what to say to Mr. Knight.
He had told me to be quiet but now he wanted me to talk.

I sat on my side of the tent and sewed.

Sometimes I read the book by Frederick A. Cook.
It had been thrown across the tent at me.

In that moving world of ice...an ascertainment of actual
position...is...impossible—
*My Attainment of the Pole Being the Record of Expedition that
First Reached the Boral Center*— Frederick A. Cook—

Therefore, the accomplishments of many explorers throughout
history have been doubted.

I read what Cook wrote about hunting the musk ox.
I read his words about the dogs, the sledges, the cold,
the Eskimos— implacable and heartless, but capable of
indomitable courage, persistence, and dogged hopefulness.

Now I stood over Mr. Knight crying.
He was sick a long time.
I didn't think he would live as long as he did.
I didn't want him to go, no matter how mean he had been to me.

## 12.

When I did not hear Mr. Knight move, I leaned over to hear
his breath.
I listened.
I nudged him.
He didn't move, but I knew he was still alive.
I sat by him.
Vic sat with him, too.
I needed to hunt, though Mr. Knight was beyond wanting food.
I sat with him another day.
In the evening, when I touched his body, it was not warm.
He had died quietly— without my notice.

That night, I heard the spirits.
Vic growled.
I told her to be quiet.

I slept— I woke. A man stood before me in a bear-hunting suit—
a leather coat and trousers covered with spikes. He wore an
iron helmet covered with nails. He looked like a bristly walrus.
He held an ice pick in one hand. A harpoon in another. A light
shined from his snow goggles. I could not move. When he
dropped the harpoon, he held the moon in his hand, small as a
duck egg. Polar bears circled the moon. The man was a nomad
now— cleared of scurvy and abandonment— an iron beast
rolled in from the next world.

It was another lesson of Wrangel Island.

13.

I couldn't dig a grave.
The ice was hard.
I didn't have a shovel.
I stood outside in the cold.
I looked to the inlet for a ship.
I called into the wind.
I stood until I was shaking.
My knees buckled.
I crawled back inside the tent.
Victoria licked my face.
I would leave Mr. Knight in his deerskin sleeping bag.
It would not take long for his body to freeze.

14.

Two ravens followed me one day. Squawking.
They told me their stories were older than mine.
They were the ones that belonged on the island.
Not us.
Not me.

Where was rescue?
The men had looked through the field glasses for a ship.
Now I looked.

My rescue was the Lord— I thought of him on the cross when I
saw the logs of driftwood.

I remembered the men packing the dog sled.
I knew they would leave me alone with Mr. Knight.

What would I do?

I was not taught to hunt and fish.
If I was with my father, he did the work.
Let me go with you— take me with you— I would beg— and
he took me in the sled wrapped in skins and mukluks and a
parka—
the fur of the hood blowing across my face.
My gloves so thick I couldn't push the fur away.
It all was one— the land the sky the water.

Father Father, I cried in the Methodist Mission.
Your father is in heaven, they said. God is your Father now.
God in Jesus Christ.
I cried and cried in my bed.

The missionaries sat with me.
Father Father, take me with you, I said.
The missionaries gave me an orange, like the sun when it went
down for the long winter night.

I remember learning to write the letters of the alphabet
at the Methodist Mission.

ADA DELUTUK
A was the pointed breath of an elk in frigid weather.
D had the rounded belly of the elk.
E was the whiskers.
L the leg of an elk.
U the curve of the mouth.
T the tail.
K the antlers.

I kept the Bible by my bed—
a gun, sewing needles, sinew, knitting yarn, knife.

In the Arctic you don't know where you are or what day it is.
You believe in spirits.
You are taken from yourself.
Similar to nothing.

Sometimes I thought the spirits were pawing my sleeping bag,
but it was Victoria, the cat.
Vic, I called her now, as the men had called her.

I dreamed I was on the edge of the ice.
Digging roots.
Digging for writing— or what the letters meant when they
were joined with others— and whatever the words meant

when they were together in a sentence.
I liked to see how they could change in relationship to the
other words they stood by.

Writing at first was like scratching in the snow.
The paper was white as the snow.
I could say writing was like an elk digging for roots.
Scratching with its hoof and nose.

I am not alone.

I made a little calendar book for 1923.
I cut typing paper into pages and drew boxes for each day of
the month.
I marked them off when they passed.
I looked at the days I had marked off.
They flew away as birds.

I am not alone.
I have a diary.
I am not alone.
Vic, the cat, is with me.

I am delirious at times.
When you are alone you look at your hands as if they are not
yours.

Jesus is there more than the writing, the missionaries would
have said.

How do I inhabit the words that inhabit the past?
I feel it when I write.
The past is somewhere under the words.

I want to turn the page in my little book and see where the past is hiding.
But the other side is only blank until I write on it.
The spirits of the animals are there, too.

The air is silent.
The cold is silent.
Vic is silent.
To write words is to make marks that are not marks in themselves but carry another.
Writing refers to others.
It becomes others.
Making words is a dog sled over the snow.

Writing words finds roots in the ice.
It combines with other words in useable parts.
A slight curve in the writing makes another direction to carry words back to camp.
I am hunting when I am writing.
Letters are animals.
You find them and shoot them and they fall before you.
I record what I hunted.
How many ducks I saw pass.

The repetition each day eating— expelling what the body lets out.
We are ruled by the body.
Its hunger.
Its demands.
Keeping it warm.
Keeping it fed.
Bearing its dying.
But there are the thoughts, also— buzzing in the top of the world.

I am hurting when I am writing.

In the silence in the tent I heard it hum— the silence that
writing is.
It does not make noise— except a small *shrifff* across the
paper.

Mr. Knight would have heard it—
if he was not dead in his sleeping bag.

What are you writing? he would have asked.
He knew the journey of words on paper.
The world is writing its story on us.
We are writing our story on it.

15.

I am not alone.
The headache is with me.
I am not alone.
The sky is with me.
The crowded stars.
They are not alone.
Have there ever been so many?

The waves of Polar Lights move across the heavens.
Back and forth. Back and forth.
Wandering forever and ever.
They should make camp.
But they have to keep moving.
They are restless.
What are they looking for?
Maybe they are hungry, too.

The north is full of light.
Even in darkness.
Even in soundlessness there is sound.
The hum of the world below rises to the top.
The sniffing of the tails of light and dark as they move around
each other.

The sound of a polar bear padding across the snow.
The fear of seals when they sense it coming.

What is this moving in me?
Three men gone to Siberia do not come back.
I still sew for them.
Lorne Knight is dead.

I dream of ice that has nothing on it.
I am not alone.
The churning thoughts are with me.
When I sleep, others are with me.
I'm not sure who they are.
My children.
My sister.
My father and mother.
The ones who came before them.
As I wake, they leave.
Slowly at first.

The words I write stretch across the page like a trap-line map.
I let the letters walk away from one another until they are not
where they belong.

16.

Sometimes I hear the three explorers who left for help.

If I look from the flap of the tent, they are not there.

I see the snow circling between the tent and the row of barrels.

I hold my ears when the wind blows.
*WOOOOOOOOOOOOOOOOOOOOOOOOOOOOOOOOOOOOOO—*
For days, the wind blows.

I know the men are dead.
They are dead.
But they call from somewhere— tangled in the wind.

## 17.

Crawford, Maurer, and Galle took most of the instruments with them.
I use the gun and knife they left.
I look for seals, white fox, birds.
I belong to the Arctic.

I find in Mr. Knight's Bible—
*She is not afraid of the snow*— Proverbs 31:21

I do not think of you enough, Lord.
I have ignored you.
Now I need you.

A cloud crosses the sky.
A distant ridge of ice crosses an inlet of Wrangel Island.
The island is a whale floating in the Arctic Sea.

*I am a sojourner on the earth*— Psalm 119:19.
*My soul clings to the dust. Revive me according to your word*—
Psalm 119:25.
When I read the Psalm I say, *My soul clings to the ice. My soul freezes for heaviness*— Psalm 119:28.
*It is good for me that I have been afflicted, that I might learn thy statutes*— Psalm 119:71.
Otherwise, I would not think of God.

Jesus was tied to the cross.
I was tied to a flagpole when Mr. Knight was alive.

After Mr. Knight died, I am careful turning the pages of his Bible.

Maybe it is Mr. Knight's grandfather I feel with me.
Or his father.
Mr. Knight, also.
The men to whom the pages belong. Maybe the stars, too.

When I am alone with myself, there is another there—
not the frozen body of Mr. Knight in his deerskin bag.
Not the polar bear.

It is the spirits that are there.
They spark the air with ice.

The animals have their own world.
A world within a world.
It is a belonging we share.

At night— what is it touching me?— The stars?
My two dead children?

It is an unknown world that moves around me.

18.

The driftwood tells stories of where it came from.
One piece looks like a fish.
Another, a bird.

I found a piece of driftwood with nail holes.
It had been part of an old ship that sank.
I laid the piece over a longer piece and made a cross.
It was crooked.
But it was there on the shore.

Once I see the driftwood from a distance
and think it is the explorers.
I run to it and see it is not the men.

The driftwood is part of Wrangel Island.
No one will come for it.

19.

I hear his breath as I sew.
But when I look in his direction,
I know the body of Mr. Knight is not breathing.

Later, I go out and see a fox with a trap on its leg.

It got into the springlock on the oil cans
and the trap caught on its leg.

I see the fox again the next day.

I set more traps.

Now I catch the fox with the trap on its leg.

Breath is nothing more than thread that follows a needle
through a piece of hide or cloth.

20.

I saw a little white owl.

It reminded me of a blank page in my diary.
Or a square not yet marked off in my calendar book.

I know there are roots under the snow.
If only I could reach what I am,
I could survive alone on Wrangel Island.

The men had been cruel to me.
Their words were knives.

Their silence now was fire.

21.

I sew crooked stitches for a line of driftwood
on the bottom of my parka.
When I sew, I stitch my fretting into the threads.
The stitches hold the pieces together.

Jesus was sewed on the cross.
I think of him often.

It snows.
The wind blows.
I go outside and fix the stove pipe.

I clean skins. I sew gloves and slippers for Bennett.

I make soles for new felt boots— another collar on my coat—
I twine cords for decoration—
I make scalloped edges and jagged elk-tooth patterns for my
reindeer parka—
I wash clothes.
I mend my yarn gloves.

I sew the wind, but it doesn't hold still.

I sewed the tent to the ground.
I sew Wrangel Island to the air above the water.

I feel alone, as I did after my father died.
I push back the fear and distress.
My stomach hurts.
My head hurts.

My words hurt.
My sewing hurts.

I sew another collar on my blanket coat.
I chew the hide to make it softer.

Victoria still chews the fox skin for something to eat.

I sew another parka.
I knit the fingers of Maurer's gloves that he would never wear—
and do more fancy sewing for the parka.

I make a canvas boat.
I make two paddles for the canvas boat.

Rain and wind this morning.
When I go for more driftwood, I fall in the water on the edge
of the harbor just to my ankle.

I cut a little pile of driftwood.
I leave it by the stove.
Vic likes to shuffle through it and find a little place to nap.

I am not alone.
I am a seamstress.

What if I run out of thread?
What if I run out of writing?

22.

The wind howls at night. The storm has come back. I feel Vic burrowing into my sleeping bag. I am not the men she prefers, but she stays close to me now. I feel her heart racing. I join her in prayer.

23.

Once I heard a story of a girl who found the skull of a man.
Her father threw it in the water. She went to find it. She saw
a man in the water, but he did not want her. He told her to
walk to a fork in the road. If she took the left fork she would
return to her father and mother. But the left road was hard
and she took the right. She walked until she came to the
moon. Someone told her there was an old woman in a cabin
who would not let the man in the moon get her. A bear was
in front of the cabin. The girl was afraid but if she turned
back, the man in the moon would get her. The bear growled
but didn't eat her. The old woman took a plank from the floor.
The girl looked down and saw all the people walking there.
The old woman said if she wanted to go home, she had to sew
several pairs of mittens. She threw a rope from the moon to
the earth. The girl put on some mittens and climbed down.
When the mittens wore out, she would put on another pair.
The old woman told her to keep her legs straight when she
reached earth. If she curved her legs, she would be old when
she reached earth. When the girl got close to the earth there
was nothing to do but drop from the rope. She hurried to her
mother and father's house, but it was gone.

What did that story mean?
How did the skull become a man?
How did the land become water?
Where was the path that led to the moon?

It was like sewing when I didn't know what kind of stitches my
needle would make.
It was like words I wrote that made a pattern of their own.

It was like the driftwood that transformed the shore of the
island.
I thought sometimes I could hear its voice.

The story of the girl meant that nothing was certain.
It meant I lived in a drifting world.
It meant everything was possible.

24.

But what if no one comes?
What if another winter is ahead?

I typed on Galle's typewriter.

i land
is land

It is paper that is water.

Vic stuck it out as I typed, though I propped the tent door
open for her with a small tin.

25.

One day after I cleaned a seal, I heard a noise outside the door.
There was a polar bear and her cub.
I fired over their heads.
They ran a little ways and turned back and looked at me.

Vic came out from behind the stove.

Another morning, I opened the door and found a large polar
bear track outside the tent.
The next day the bear ate all the seal oil.

I couldn't sleep at night until I read for a while. I remembered
in the Methodist mission, if I didn't read, I liked to turn the
pages of the book.

One evening, I thought I heard a noise like a boat whistle.
I thought it was a bird.
Maybe it was the owl I saw.

The next morning I heard the noise again.
I looked through my field glasses.
And there was a BOAT.
Men were walking toward the beach.
I went to meet them.

A man asked where the men were and I told him I was the only
one left.

The rescue ship came two years after we arrived on Wrangel
Island.
I was alone on the island two months after Mr. Knight died.

I showed the man my calendar book.

The men buried Mr. Knight's body and left a marker.
They packed the few supplies that were left and the garments I
made— the gloves and boots, an embroidered coat, slippers for
Bennett, a reindeer parka.

I wrapped my writings, my sewing thread, needles, and
thimble in a seal-skin bag.

I carried Victoria to the boat in a meal sack with her head
poking out.
She didn't struggle.
She seemed to know we were leaving.

———————

In the end, Wrangel Island was claimed by Russia.

———————

# PART TWO

---

ADA'S WRITINGS AND DIARY

*No man sews a piece of new cloth on an old garment: otherwise,*
*the new piece pulls away from the old, and the rent is made worse*
   *— Mark 2:21*

*In transferring the scanned text of Ada's unpublished writings into a Word program, some of the lines are missing or misaligned. Some of the lines tore. The old words did not fit the new margins. Yet a splicing was done. Renting the old. Leaving scars. I left the lines as they are—unreadable in places.*

*The oddities that happened in the disruptive transfer of Ada's diaries to Word left tearings or rip-lets in Ada's text. It was the same ripping the explorers experienced when they arrived on a barren island with a plan for the arrival of a supply boat and sufficient game for survival, and found the plan did not fit the actuality. It was the same rift-lines between Ada's text and my interpretation of the undertext I found in her writings.*

*But the story here is about the new patterns that show up in the middle of disruption. The blurred passages are the history we try to recreate but cannot meet the exact happenings. There is the arrival of the unforeseen. The old was in place. Then came the new cartographies on top of the earth. A splicing that would not work. Yet the work was done.*

# Rauner Special Collections Library PDF Scanning Request

Dartmouth College • 6065 Webster Hall, Hanover, NH 03755
rauner.reference@dartmouth.edu • TEL: (603) 646-0538 • FAX (603) 646-0447

| Name: | |
|---|---|
| Email Address: | |
| Mailing Address: (for billing) | |
| Type of Copy (Circle one):     COLOR PDF SCAN          PAPER PHOTOCOPY | |
| Fee (Circle one): DC ON-SITE (.10/scan          HER ON-SITE (.25/scan) FF-SITE (.50/scan) | |

CHART STRING

| | | |
|---|---|---|
| | | |
| | | |
| | | |
| | | |
| | | |
| | | |
| | | |
| | | |
| | | |

| | | |
|---|---|---|
| | | |
| | | |
| | | |
| | | |
| | | |
| | | |
| | | |
| | | |
| | | |

Staff Initials: MSwan

Dartmouth College Library e Rauner
Special Collections Library
RAUNER LIBRARY
MATERIAL REQUEST FORM

## MANUSCRIPT MATERIAL

For this request to be processed, you MUST provide the following information about the item you are requesting
from our collection.

ITEM INFORMATION
Please supply information for
EITHER (I) OR (II)

(1) INDIVIDUAL
MANUSCRIPT

FALL 1921

ition.

Fall of I92I

Sent        exploring        part        v        to
Wranglle Island.Arrived in Nome,Alaska,
Sent ember T st, T 921, and v;ere looking for a
seamstress to t 'A-e alcng with them, v.$^r$ hereby
U; , S, Marshall Jcrdon, introduced A d?
Bleckjack to Crawford, who w?.s head of tae
Eynec)ition. Dnring their short stav in 1101-ne
they Chertered the boat. Silver W?.ve, the
commanders name l'!as Jack Hammer, who had snent
many veers in the Artic Waters.

Before we 1 e? t I bonght some sinet', needle,
thimble and some linen thread. l'!e left Ilome about
Sept e.Lber 0 , T 9 ET , and 2 rrived at Wrangle T
sland September 16th, T 921. On our wav to
Wrangle Island we stonned on Ace Cane to cet some s
invc and white seal skin, we also bought a small Eskimo
skin boat. After wye left Ace Cape, about six hours out
t ne engine broke down ard we had to lay over About a
half dav and n i Eåt.

',Vhen we got to Vlrangle I s lard, the main 1
and looked very 1 arge to me, 'out they said tåat it
was only a small T slande T thought at first that T
would Orn back, T decided it wouldn' t, be f air to
the bovs so T ? e lt that T hod to stay. Soon after
we arrived T started to sew on some snow shirts for
t he we bronpht some Reindeer Skin Perkes and a 1 T
T he d to do was to fasten the hoods on to them, for
it was verv cold end the T)oys fi+eded them to a
17,011 t

They use to haul lots of 'trooö to cret wood
l?iJes for the v! inter, they made the frame t cr the
snow house for v; i pter end about the l?.st •ort of

69

October thev pnt the snow blocks in, we were living
in a tent ? t •first and it v;as rather comcl .

The first fall oh"-y one of the boys was
trapping fox. he was the on J v one that T know of
that was tranning. After Christmas the rest of the
bovs did some tranping but T don ᵗ t think they cot
many fox thoueh. Just L ecore Christmas two a f the
boys, Maurer and Crtwford, went to t ne East o? our
oarnp. T dcn' t know how many foy they got, they
didn ᵗ t get many though for they didn't hatre bait Q
for fox,

' ! hen 3 or ing came In 192? , we saw some geese
and ducks, then we had some vood meat. That s or ing
tae boys €0 t over 30 e eaTs, and over TO polar bears
all teget6er 1 nclud ing the      ones      mothers.Not
many of' the skins could be used for the weather was so
damp and we had no way to    them,   so  only  one  or  two
were saved.

The surnzner 19?0?, ten 1 ght took trip to the East
our  camp,  ebon  t  60  miles  that  he  seid  he  erossed  a
river cal. led
   Skeleton Äiver, which he had to swim across. Fe said it
wae quit, e ▨ large river. H f ter he came 'Dtzck the
other three boy g left to take the
• same trip. C. f ter his trip Knight was never well,
corm) a ined of a sore back and said he felt we?k.
V!hen Knirht took 1, he trip he took a dog Q Tong to
carry  his  small  things.  While  the  other  were  away
Mr.Knight, k i 1 Ted a biff no 112. r hear, lyot, we
didn't touch the meat for

We didn't care for it because we had dnckg end geese
and bran t. After the bovs came hone, Yao rer sqäd he
we..s '70 inc to fry some of time bear ▨▨meat, but T
never cared for it before, because it, tasted strong,
but in thet summer of 1922 the bear meat tasted fine, it
tae ted ill st Tike beaf—steak to me for we had had no
meat for. sonle time.   fried some of the nomar ¹oeQY'

blvbber and "0 t one barrel, one coal oil tin
and one twenty-five pound lard tin full, this oilis verv
good.The
    use that oil to f r tr the hard b ÆQd in, it is verv
    flood , IV-it T couldn't hardly eat it beceose it
    tasted so strong to me   the t 1 me.

        g f ter the borrs c? me on thev k i T Ted another
    polar bear, oh'. he was so fat. Then they saw sone we J
    rus out In the broken ice, they went out after them and got
    two o? them. They had a E I G? t, deal of trouble getting
    the. meat to shore. They couldn't get the boat to where
    the was, sc thev took sled end put the mett on it and when
    they y-•ere crossing two ice cares the sled got between
    the ice colres ftnd tipoed over, They lost all of the meat
    in t, he v:ater, but they saved some 06 it hilt, not ail.

        We were expecting a boat ever'.r F ay t, bat evmmer,
    (1922) because some times the ocean clears so t hat the
    boats cart come in, the ice goes out but comes in again,
    It cleared out the most the summer of 1923, when thetr
    rescned me. In ? t)out 19?? I was wondering how far out
    the ice 'tras into the ocean, eo I t hooch t some dav T
    would take trip out there and see, we 1 7 one I decided
    to take this trip, so T started end I "0 t, vinst to the
    toot o? moon tain When heavy fog came u 1? and ni<ht fall
    together T had to turn back, and I didn't find out how
    far out the ice was or ran.

        The boys expected a boat up until the last of
    October. Around about November they new the boat wouldn't
    come. About the middle of November we moved up to the
    west of our present camp, about four miles I think, so
    they wouldn't have to haul the wood so far. After we arri
    ved in our new camp I started to sewing skins for the two
    boys, Knight and Crawford, who were going to take a trip
    to Siberia. They were preparing therest of their things
    and helping to haul wood so the other

    boys would not have so much to do after they left.

At Christmas time we had some Salt seal meat and
some hard bread and tea for our Christmas dinner. That
time when we had dinner I won— dered where I would be if
I lived until next Christmas. After Christmas about
January 8th, the boys, Knight and Crawford, left for
Siberia. They came back about the 21 of January, they
were only gone about 13 days, for Knight became sick and
they had to turn back. When they gpt back Knight vas
very sick and weak. Then they talked about the other
three boys taking the same t rip to Siberia, and Knight
said it would be better because the three boys could
make a camp, a snow house, easier

at night than two boys could. So about January 28th the
three boys, Crawford, Maurer and Galle, left for Si beria.
They promised that they would come back after they got to
Nome, with a boat and if they couldn t t get there with a boat
they would come over with a dog team next winter. They left
with a team of five dogs and a big sled of supplies. After
they left I started to do some tramping. After about one
week, Knight seemed to be getting along alright, he could
chop a little wood, but after a week he had to bring some
wood in the tent to chop and while choping it he fainted, and
was unconcious about five minutes. He was so weak that I told
him he had bet ter stay in bed, that I could chop the wood
and bring in the snow for water. 1 told him I was use to
choping wood and doing that kind of work down home, so he
finally consented to let me.
   . I went out to Maurer'sttrap line, before he left he
had given Mr. Knight his trap line map, when I went out
the first day I only found about six or seven of the
traps, but later on about three or four days afterwards
I found the rest, but there were no fox in any of them.
1 trapped for about a month but I never caught a fox.
   When I was out I was afraid of meeting a polar bear
and every little while I would turn and look around to
see if one was in sight and if there had of been one, I
would have fainted, for I only had a snow knife with me
and I didn't know what to do to defend myself, • for I
never carried a rifle when out on the trap line. I went
out every dau for I knew I had to get something to eat
for Knight was sick and we had •nothing in the tent. I

just got weak from trarap ing aroUnd and I thought I
would give it up, but one day I noticed some fox tracks
around one of the traps so I dug the trap out of the
snow, for in setting the fox traps up there you bait
them and then cover them with a little snow, but I guess
I covered them to much and that is the reason Why I
didn&t get any fox, then I baited it again end just left
it on top Of the snow didn't cover it up at all. The
next morning I got up and looked out and I saw a fox, I
didn't know for sure if it was in the trap or not, but I
dressed and went over and sure enough it was a white fox
in my trap and that was the first one I had caught, and
that was on the ZZnd of February, 1923. After that I
caught some more. in March I caught quite a few, one day
I caught three. In killing them I would take a stick and
hit them on the head until I stunned them then I would
bend their heads back until I broke there heck.   Then I
would take them home and skin them.

        Later in the spring, around April the fox got very
scarce,  and  I  couldn't  trap  and  more  at  all.  After  I
couldn't get any more fox, Knight became worse he got very
faint every time he moved. I for got to tell you that none
of us had ever eaten a white fox before but I remembered
off reading in a book that the people up North said that
they were very good to eat so when I caught the first one
we tried it, and liked it very much. Around about May, I
think, I took a walk across the other direction, towards
the small Islands in the harbor, and a sea gull flew over
my head, I had brbught a shot gun With me this time, one .
that belonged to Knight, and I took a shot at it with my
gun and killed it, I took it home and made some broth with
it for Elight for he could eat very little. That was the
first bird I ever shot with a shot—gun. I have shot them
with a twenty—two rifle dovm home but never with a shdt
gun.

        One morning about the 10th of May I think, I woke up
and heard something dripping and • I thought it was the
water dripping from the tent , so I got up and I saw that
it was Knights nose bleeding, he had a one

pound tea tin half full of blood from his nose. He had
been bleeding for some time, it was about ten o'clock in

73

the morning when I found hem, His face was just blue, he
turned his face away from the can and he looked just like
he was dead, he was half dead. I called him four or five
times before he answered, then he said he was better. I
ask him if he would eat some hard bread soaked in oil and
fried, he said he would so I fixed him some, for that was
all that we had. That was the day that I got the sea gull.
The next morning he said that he felt much better so I
cooked the sea gull and gave him some of the broth. Around
in February when he first got sick he gave me his Bible
which belonged

to his Grandfather.
    Llonrr in June about the first v,ᴿ eek T t cok a walk to
the west of onr camp : and when T was comIrv back across the
harbor    T    noticed  something like that, t  some sea gum 7 alo
the   beach    and   T   , and I found one egg.  wondered      Y/ået
thev  had,   I   thon  ded not to wast any mo  57b  t nerhens it
was    some    walrus                          meat,  or  but,  T
got there T fonffd they were 'cuiTc3inv a nest,Y tried to k i
T T some of them but couldn' t so decided not to more t i!ne
, T had one egg, for the n i t anv wav. Y'ihile on the rest
c? my wav home across the lake some v: hit e geese flew over
rav heed , T took a shot at them thew went cn for about one
hundred feet then one of them dræ»ed and I enre v.'as glad.
So when T got hone T called to V-iight, ᵗᵗ lcok v:hat I vot ᵗ'
, he onened his evee end said ᵗ' v;hat i  and ne sea ge wæ-
ted to kn o— the, e, and told him it was l.varrn •t:hen f
cund it, so T fried it for him, but first T to break- it i
nto a to show him it v.es fresh. cooked the v: i 7.13 roose
nntiT the iG? t f e 17 € rom the bone for had verv few teeth
thetr were out f' rom sour v 'T, nine more in the seme rest,
ete thoee e •r s *'hi Ye he T i vinc beezv.se he dn' t eat on
?.ccov.nt of' hie throat be inc: so sore.
    •a        of' water.
stand to keen his feet         every        night for two months


        three cr he ? ere tie d led, hr d to make a from
cot meal and f i -u led it T/ ith cot t, cn t e put under his
back zee'. '1 se he sz. :-d

that T would find t, he kev to his •trunk in his

                                        200k
                                        et, he
                                        Elec
                                        told
                                        them

  Abcnt, the         before he died I knev,' t rat he cry-Il dn ᵗ t 'l
Tist much


          'LIS t cov.ldn ' t  b'.lt or v for I knew he wotÜdn'
t              'Ant i T

                                    ?
rrived, f ovnd him (3 e? c? the  z? ter
he gaw me ervlng.
                          the n i r ht. A f ter he
died wrote Tetter him y•r hat day, month the cance o?
Tlnichts deeth, beet" se T thon "'hkt something ml "h t to
me, then thev wouldn't ʰ im, beeevse a an i mal or
scnethinr; m i "h t vet me I)efore the 130 at err 1 lured
. also "!rot e 7 etter to lir e Who T t ho;vht, T Yet %
the letters in the t, v nevriter go if T not there l'!hen
t, he bon t arrived the " find the letters and know c f'
our neat, as. T Tett Yr. Knight in the tent for T could not
him, T moved into another one that we had ' l sea moetTv•
for e t, or in things in.

    Three davs after Mr. Kni-ht died I got some seal, about
and a week aft erv,'hrds T got a other seal. T shot rifle.
those - v: ith KnightsSo one dav we•it out a ᵣ:ain , it
was the 4th J LOY, (T made a calendar out of t v nevvrit-
in,' na:ner cut into small oiecee, I one for 1922, but T
had to msyke my IPE3 ctlendar T st i T I have in trunk.)
Then went to ret my t h 1 rd seal 1 craw 1 i v, r •-1 ong
on my stomach to pet ᴍᴘ c Ibse enough to shoot it and T
VIP. s just re;a.dyr to s i 111 when it moved so t hat a
ice cake extended in front or between me and the e eal, so

  I was moving around to get a better        end T had ? in.ger on
the •

hamı'îıer ,     i r r:zoving T mı-ıst h? ve puılled it     B-J)ᵀG ! vuᶠent t
he gun and      v.;ent thf?   i n tı n t h e? water T ö i ön ' t ge t     men
t .
T nthought , well , T h mır 4 th of    eel?brpt iorı

    T'he    vı.7S on Iv a f ev: var de from the    mv t en t .
t hir•ö sen I 'T got T -ıvent 071 t 12bcuıt two varös
on t î rom t h? beach t, he i ce a sezi, so T we.'?t
ont to t ak e ?hot '3 t got t his T t 30 far 01-1 t t
hat T knew -y - 9 t it to t h? tept 7 i t h 017 t sone
t to me, T v;ent to t, he tert rot a I i re î cr t her
stnrted "f ter Y -en r 1 v to it Ioukeö sone t hirg t
hat locked ,jvıst like a ve 1 lor: hali cominz•
tor;zrds me, fi nallv T repljzeö i t 'oear
    Y fren       tent e     T turned end hard as I
coııld       T çot te ten t , T       r ep.öv to
    I got t here ta. I bu IT t '3. high Y' T f t ot t
he hack o î m v ter t clinbed onto this tock mv fi eld
glnsses and V'? t,checl tiıe bee.r her one e- t rnv
sepi Fit leest I thomrht She Y t f "Ta Y I y rot so I
öeciöeö I tıp ö bet t er not te.ke chance aft er it t
h' t n 1 rht so 'N?iteö t he next ıııorrıin:z ovıt ü
ook Iook, -c:vıt mg grene , t hat left a f eı.pı blöod
marks. The molıher ö her I ? t er came to ? boııt
onehundreö an d fiftv yer53 îrom t he ten t .

    Oneözv Ön s t aft er T hafi my sez I hep rö a 20
i ge ,jUIFt like dog 011 t si de of rıv door T 1 cokeö
on t t de öoor and 2 bovıt fi f teen feet îrom t he
tent El g beşi r and yovı.ng one, T very ece,red, but
T took my r i fle ?.nd t hoı-ırht take 2 chşınce,
1 î T i 1.1 3 t hit t hen i
n t he î 00 t             pfter me, so I fired over their heads
or sone pi ace and ran   ways and turned and looked as if the
pıhere      it   so I     more shots at them and they ran awa
woıılfi on I y i n j'nre t hem II t t 1? t hey
vıcı,21d andthey tu•rned a 11 t t le ouldc c:ıe back î
ireö f ive for good t hen.

    One morning after T fi2ö bu ilt fire T opened t he öoor
a 7 Fırge polar 'oepr trpek riçht i ᵞ-? th9 öcor      I
091 t      I cokeö andhe h? d 'ne en 211 around ıt he
tent.   T har?   tıventy—îive _nouırıd 12Td tin of o il

on t s Ide oî mır ten t and about three    n f tee t he f
Irst beer had been t here another benr came ene ni?ht
    P. te 311 of thet t i n of ö i 1 I tdi22k it        on
iv one  the tracks ? IT Tookeö t he    size.

evening about

t âe TP t h of Auqııst , T makinç; rry Ivınch or  ard a funny
supper, T hettrd noise I j ke b0?t rıh is t 1 e, but t
hovıç;ht  it 2 duck  or eonıetiıing, it wes foggv T
covıldn' t eee so T ö i d n 't t hink any more şibovıt it
vın til t he next mornirg I took my book 2 î t er supper,
for T com lön' t go to e leep nntil T had reeö for
a while, t hen I ıvent to s leep, The 22?Yt nornirış;
zboat si x o' clock T hearö that sama more like a boz t
whistle t his tine 30 1 vıent
011 t on top of my reft, e.nd sure enoug-h there vıas
a boa t the mester andt he F; ere on t he beack. T h?iö
on Ty sone .tea for break f 23 t t hat mor n i ne for
watc(ıed t he bot! t see i î t hey vvere
50 ing to oo:ne 1-1 p to my c?fflT. I t hotıght it Pli
göt be Ö vıst boa t , ö I İn 't knovv vıhat to do, but t
he bopt F t art ed n p towprds my tent T suıre tickled. I
v,ᶜ ent to t he beech to rneet the 130? t , t masta er
;yrhich Native ceme t o where t he r eğ? t of th•e v: ere
I t clö h i 21 there i'lere ro more t h? t T t he ehon Iy
one lef t .
    T .Gidn' t know v;hat to say to him; T was so tick Ted.
    T told him t h? t T "'as elone, that    Yr i c•ht had
died end that the others had gone to Siberia, and esk
him if he had not hear from them in 1.'ome , but, he
said th2t Stef tasson had sent him after them, so I
told him they were rone, that T was the only one Jett,
    The next day they buried Tlr. Knigfor T told them that
I had not.

    Ve staid there a boyIt two or three dt.rs, they were
unloeding the hoat they had brought a lot o? suoplies for the
peovle that are u r. there now.
They had brought supp) i es for two years but were on) v son
ᵞ)oserl to one winter.

    The only letter T had got fron George Ely was the one
that I got on that bop t. T was expecting letters from my

77

sister but that was the only one that T got whim e T was
   there.    As soon as I saw some of the boys from Nome, on
the boat T ask them how Benne t,      little boy, was and they
s? i d he was fine.   I hr.r3 T oft him in Yome in a Home
where he had been for some time before T left on this trip.

     ᵛ'e sailed for Yome ? rom Wranglie on the 23rd of kugust,
the last day 01⁰ ᵣᵤₛₜwe got to Yome, and Vy sister told me
that they he? rd at, • Nome that wex were all dead up ? t
Wranglle, and I guess that is Y"öy rny sister did not ᵂ⁴write
to me. T don' t know what happendd to the boys that left for
Siberia, I h? ve never heard anv word of them since. ᵗ$lhen T
carne book 1 found out that my Stepfather had died. sister
had harl baby while i was gone '"hen she heard t h? t we I-r
ere dead ehe npmer7 the baby after me. The I.ᵀ ative boys that
were working, cn the '002 t Danielson i that came up there
ₐₙд"0 t me, told me that, if Mr. Yo i ge had not I)een Oeptian
t,hev heye turned back long before they got to V!ranglleIsla

                                                          1•
                                                          wa
                                                          nt
                                                          to
thank Mr. No ice manv•, many times for saving mylife, for I am
sure the t T would not have been alive now if he hadn't, and I
will always remember it. Although it wag no ones fault but my
own that I went up there for no one would have f D    me to •o
but T wanted to go and thQ'2ght I would never have another

                              *respectfully,*
chance to go so I took it. dint

                              ØZDo
                              *Ada Black jack*

RAUNER LIBRARY MATERIAL REQUEST FORM

## MANUSCRIPT MATERIAL

For this request to be processed, you MUST provide the following information about the item you are requesting from our collection.

ITEM INFORMATION

Please supply information for EITHER (I) OR (II)

(1) INDIVIDUAL MANUSCRIPT

Collection Name

Manuscript Number:

(Location), if any:

ONE          NUMBER
ONLY.

See examples, below.     See examples, below.

_____          _____

Frost                              961232.1

Last and
most complete
Transcription

Ada Blackjack's Diary

1923

**Made in March 14th, 1923.** The fox I caught was in feb. 21st and then second March 3 and 4th, 5th, that makes 4 white foxess and then in March 13th I caught three white foxess that makes seven foxess altogather. 14th I ·got headach all day I t m taking aspirin its seems didn't work. Oh yes in 13th I got new army pans. On 12th of Mar. I site eight placeses of traps two in each place.

**15th**. I was over to the traps no sign of fox fresh tracks. And I put new sole on my felt slipers and was the dishess and I feel much better than yesterday. Very clear al day.

**March 16th**. I have not feeling well for three day Crist I was headach and then I had stumpick trouble and today I feel much better. I was over to the traps with no fox or fresh tracks. *Cmd last night knight told me I can keep the bible he siad he give them to me, very nice day so far.

**Mar. 18.** I caught one male fox today fat one too, and I cut little part of my si·ck (?) and mail the piece of reindeer skin and then I wash my head. Oh yes I got snow glasses today and I dug the tirep out and put it in the storm shiet hight told me to take in.

**March 19th**. I was over to the traps and found thqt fox has been in trap and she run away with the trap the one that is by cold oil can and I haul two sled load and chop wood and I found slat it was ____(?) last of those two boxess. And I open the case of distillate.

**20**<sup>th</sup>. I caught one male fox today fat one too.

**21**<sup>st</sup>. I caught one female fox and I haul one sled load and chop wood. I make new sleep bokek. Yesterday I sete two more traps at cold oil can.

**22**<sup>st</sup>. One female fox I caucht today, its tisd like chicken, and I stard to make black belt for myself and I made about six inch long. 25th. I over to the traps and fox run away with three traps and then I put two traps in place of three and I haul two Slad load of wood and chip wood and this evening I work on belt about six inch long. Yesterday the fox that have trap in the foot has been around to the traps in front of camp.

**24**<sup>th</sup>. I was over to the traps today no sign of xi fox. and I work on beach and I got more then half finish.

**25**<sup>th</sup>. I didn't go out today its blowing hard and I work on beach and its about two thrid of belt work.

And I open can of Tea this evening.

**26**<sup>th</sup>. 1 was over to the traps today and fox has been in cold oil can traps and trap was sprung but didn't hold fox and this morning about 11 o'clock I sew a Polar bear on the ice, and I sew three foxess one with trap on her foot. And I haul one load of sled and saw four cuts of log and chop wood, and we look at hiights legs my: they are skiny and they has no more blue spots like they use to be. And I pretty near finish my black belt.

**27**<sup>th</sup>. I was over to the traps and caught one and another fox that has trap in her foot has been at the cold oil can. Oh my I feel very wake now I an feel it yesterday and today.

**28**. I caught a fox today the fox has trap in his foot. It has caught trap by trap that flanny. I saw one cut of wood and chop it. And I finish my beach belt.

**29**th. My eye swolen up and one side of face ach, it stard yesterday and today it very much ach. I caught one male fox it pretty good meat, and I saw six cut of wood and I chop only three.

**30**th. I didn't go out today and my eye is worse than yesterday and swealen both side eye.

**March 31**st. My eye is worse the yesterday and one side of my face is swelen and I took out ship poket and get borc acht and cotton and bondage.

**April 1**st. I didn't go out today because my face is swelen and my eye is pretty near close from swelen and its very ach.

**2**nd. I take ship poket out today one of my eye one that is swelen is going down a little, and one side of my throad out side of it, is hards a little. And knight wants me to go out to the traps but my eye is very ach so I cannot go out when my eye is that way becuase in evening I could bearly stand the ach of my eye and one side of head. If anything happen to me and my death is known, there is black stirp for bennett school book bag, for my only son. I wish if you please take everything to Bennett that is belong to me. I don't know how mach I would be glad to get home to folks.

**Apr. 5**th. My eye is getting better and sweling is going down.

**Apr. 4**th. My eye is just the same yesterday but my stumok was on bum, and I don't feel pain in my throad but my eyes was fogy today I haven't been out for three days.

**April 5**th. I go out today and carry snow in for water and took ship pocked out.

**Apr. 6**th. I made saw book today and chop wood and I feel better today. And I open case of biscuits. Blowing today.

**Apr. 7ᵗʰ**. Blowing al day I didn't go out today and yesterday on account of wind blowing.

**Apr. 8ᵗʰ**. I got up early this morning and then chop wood and I went out to the traps and caught one frozen fox nothigg but skin and bone and I open can of cold oil. And I finish one side yarn glove for Galle and stard another side.

**Apr. 9ᵗʰ**. I was over to the traps nothing doing only one fox track. And I take a bath this evening. Very clear, wind from every diricken. And I knite today.

**Apr. 10**. I caught one Tamale fox, very smale but its good mead. Clear and sunshine.

**Apr. 11ᵗʰ**. I was over to the traps no fox or traks. And I went to other side and saw wood and haul them home.

**Apr. 12**. I was out to the traps but there is nothing, and I went to other side and saw there cuts of wood and bring them home. And I t m sort of yarn for Gal le t s gloves.

**Apr. 15ᵗʰ**. I was to some of traps but see nothing and I fix the slade today and knight one of his leg strad to swelen again.

**Apr. 14ᵗʰ**. I was out to the traps today and got nothing but I saw fresh track behind the camp, and I open case of biscuits and cut out skin for my boot soles and I made thread out of sinnew and I gather biscuit crums togather and take them out. Very clear and sunshine

**Apr. 15ᵗʰ**. I was out the traps they was nothing and storming looking weather today. And I got my boots soles already and soak them and knight said he was feel bad.

**Apr. 16ᵗʰ**. i was out to the traps but see nothing and when I come home I starded chew my boot sole and then sew them on and I finish them by in evening. Wind from east.

**Apr. 17<sup>th</sup>.** I was out to the traps today but nothing to see but nice day. I guess knight is feel worse he didn't have tea this evening. He said he was headache.

**Apr. 18<sup>th</sup>.** I sew wood this morning frist and then I went out to the traps but there is nothing and then this afternoon I clean three foxess skins and I took four more in so I can clean them tomorrow. Cloudy and snow— ing today.

**Apr. 18<sup>th</sup>.** I clean one and put in strecher and skin other three skin foot of fox and this afternoon I haul one load of wood and chop wood didn't go to the traps but I could see them with field glasess but see nothing. Very clear.

**Apr. 20<sup>th</sup>.** I didn't go out today on account of wind blowing I just clean fox skin I clean two and put them in the stretchers.

**Apr. 21<sup>st</sup>.** I was today and haul sled load of wood and then chop wood didn't go out to the traps. And when I come in and build the fire Imight started to cruel with me, I cann l t count how many times he started to cruel at me every time he say something against me. He says BlackjJack was good man and was right in everything and was right to tread me mean. And saying I wasn't good to him he never stop and think how much its hard for women to take four mans place, to wood work and to hund for something to eat for him and do waiting to his bed and take the shiad out for him. And he menitions my children and saying no wonder your children die you never take good care of them. He just tear me into pieces when he menition my children that I lost. This is the wosest life I ever live in this world. Though it is hard enough for me to wood work and trying my best in everything and when I come home to rest here a man talk against me saying all kinds of words against me then what could I do. When I cann t t get meat that he say I wasn't trying to save he. And he say he was going to write to Nome people to fix me up. Then what could I do. Though I was hungry myself for meat and trying my best we both have no witness. If knight happen to die what will I do here in this island all alone he is laying in his bed since feburay 9th and now April 21ˢᵗ he is looks very skiny. And its long time yet till we might see ship come. Well God knows everything.

If I be Imown dead, I want my sister Rita to take Bennett my son, for her own son and look after every things for Bennett she is the only one that I wish she take my son don't let his fathar Black Jack take him, if Rita my sister live. then I be clear.

Ada B. Jack.

**Apr. 22.** I didn't go out today becuase I was just chock with cry. And then this evening I took out ship pocked. And stove ases can.

**Apr. 23ⁿᵈ.** I saw four cuts of cotton wood over to the East of camp and today I sew raven between from here and mountons. She was flying from west to east and I can not go to sleep last night untill 6 o t clock this morning and sun rise four o t clock this morning and sets fitheen minutes to nine.

**Apr. 24ᵗʰ.** I didn't go out today I just wash my hiar and read the Bibil all day and think o? folks are in church this morning and this evening and now I'm writing 11 o'c lock in evening after I had cup of tea.

**Apr. 25.** I wash my clothes today and I out and carry snow in for water. And its very clear.

**Apr. 26ᵗʰ.** I was out today and sawed wood and when I was hauling wood home I was almost fianting I guess I was so weak I was almost fianting. And this morning when I wake up from my deep sleeping I look at my watch. And t it was 4 o t clock and the inside of the house was dark so I said to myself did I sleep that long becuase I went to bed early last night, and I was thinking that we haven't enough wood for today. And I siad to myself I t 11 sleep some more untill late this evening then I'll make cup of tea and go to bed again so about 10 0' clock I zake up again it was in the morning I was glad when I know its morning.

**Apr. 27<sup>th</sup>.** Its wind blowing hard today I didn't do anything today I wasn't feeling *ell.

**Apr. 28.** Still blowing hard all day today I stay in my sleeping bag and yesterday becuase I t m not feel ling well I do nothing but reading Bible.

**Apr. 29<sup>th</sup>.** Still blowing I didn't go out. And Imight siad he was pretty sick and I didn't say nothing becuase I havo nothing to say and he got mad and he through a book at me that secont time he through book at me just becuase I have nothing to say to him. And I didn't say nothing to him and before I went in my sleeping bag I fell his water cup and went to bed.

**April 30<sup>th</sup>.** And its still wind blowing hard this last day of

**April** so knight is still living like anybody so if I happen to get back home I don't know how much I would be glad God is the only one would brought me home again. There is no one pity me in this world but God even there is no hand would help me but God, with his lovingkindness and mighty hand. May 1st. / Still blowing a little but not much, I can see sun shining throught the little hoil. And I read the noted that I write some time ago this winter about Mr. knight and its says if knimht live until May I would be glad so it happen that he still living he was just dieing in Trist part of February and now he still living untill May 1st day and if the ship comes next summer I dont t know how much I would be glad. May 2nd. Its blowing today I would go out and get wood but it was blowing so I cann't go out today.

**May 3ʳᵈ**. I was out to chop wood today and I saw snow bird. Oh my how I am glad to see snow birds come and I was out to the traps and didn't see anything even a track and I open case of biscuits.

**May 4ᵗʰ**. Wind blowing hard from west so I cann t ± go out today, well I went out to fix stove pipe. I dreamed last night that I was in land some where and knight and I was all alone and knight left for sibberia with one dog and I was left all alone. And I sew two man with dog team and I run down and ask them if they were going to Chinnik they siad they were hunding. May 5th. I was out to the traps today but see nothing and pack one sackfull of wood. Cloudy snowing and blowing .

**May 6ᵗʰ**. I was getting wood the wind blowing from north east. I didn't go out to the traps onaccount of wind blowing and I take out Polar bear oil two thrid full of tea tin.

**May 7ᵗʰ**. I was out getting wood. I didn't go out to the traps and wind blowing from west. Clear and sunshine. On thrid of May hight eat Polar bear cup paw. And I dreamed last night i was with Iöts of people and Bennett and I was looking at some pictures and we see a picture the people swiming and Bennett says swiming pool and I ask him who told you these are swiming pool pictures and he siad to me Albert told me.

**May 8ᵗʰ**. I was out just to look and see how was the weather it was cloudy braze from East. I wish I was homelso I hear people singing in Church if the Lord only carry me home I will be there some day.

**May 9ᵗʰ**. I was out this morning and I saw flock of dicks south west of camp and I was out to the traps and did not see a track of anything . And I made seal skin boats and finish the tops already to put sole.

**May 10<sup>th</sup>.** This morning when I got up Imight was nose bleeding and he ask me his can to take a dumb but he could not put the pan and I think he take a shiad in his sleeping bag and then I put the pan for him I think he was pretty near die this morning. And I was out to the traps today but did not see nothing anywhere . I was over east of camp and I sew seven Idare decke flying over me going west. And I sew sea gull way out dundra flying west, and I saw white owel. And I cut skin sole for my new boats .

**May 11<sup>th</sup>.** I was out to the traps there was nothing and I put sole on my new seal skin boats I can not sleep last night I don't know why Oh yes I put seal oil on every traps and I cut little wood. Clear and fogy and clouding vind from east.

**May 12.** I was to the traps today nothing at all. And I chop wood and haul wood and I took out some stuff from storm shad. And I fry one biscuit for hight thats all he eat for 9 days he don't look like he is going to live very long if I happen to live untill ship comes oh thank a living true God.

**May 13<sup>th</sup>.** I was to the traps there is nothing all kinds of fold of ducks flying today and old squo flies over camp cloudy and fogy and I fond ) ? ) shot gun ammunition and take them in the house.

**May 14<sup>th</sup>.** I was out to the traps there is nothing and I sew two Toolk of ducks cloudy and fogy over the mointon. And I was the dishes.

**May 15.** I was to the traps there was nothi la-light wants to go out hunding duck tomorrow.

**May 16<sup>th</sup>.** I didn't go out to the traps today and I was just getting wood and knight was nose bleeding today. And I saw snow bird and raven and I made blenked coat today.

**May 17<sup>th</sup>**. I didn't go out to the trap clear this morning and got very fogy this afternoon and I put another colar on my blanked coat and I made myself a clothe parky.

**May 18<sup>th</sup>**. I was packing wood and then I wash my clothes. Nothing to see but cloudy and fogy over the mountans and sunshine in evening.

**May 19<sup>th</sup>**. I was some more clothes of mine cloudy and snowing all day.

**May 20<sup>th</sup>**. Yesterday and last night it has been snowing about three inches deep nothing to see but cloudy and sun shining this evening. And I put new soles on my felt slipers today.

**May 21<sup>st</sup>**. I was over to the traps today nothing but raven track and I shott shot gun one time. I toök empty tea tin and shot it I shot right in it, thats pretty good for first time shooting. And I clean both shot guns.

**May 22**. didn't see nothing I didn't do nothing today.

**May 23**. I was over to little Islands to west end and some few roots I got for knight didn't see nothing but snow bird track. And I made pack for myself.

**May 24<sup>th</sup>**. I saw four flock of brant and long neck Black ducks five of them first I saw four flying south from over camp and one flying to west. All the flock of brant flying to west. And I fall in the water mouth of harper just to my Encle. And I saw one fox tracks front of camp over by big ice cake.

**May 25<sup>th</sup>**. I carry loges of about ten feet long and sawed up half of it and I saw dodlie bird flying to east and I snow bird and I shot five times with knights rifle, I did shot better then I thought I would do I only hede my target twice I thought thats good enought for me for first time shooting with rifle.

**May 26<sup>th</sup>.** I took four shott with the rifle with three first shots I didn't hided my target with the last shot I hide my target I shoot with three sitting and last one I lie on my belly. And I took a shoot with shot gun standing up and I hide my target and I made shot gun case and Imife case for myself and I saw flock of doidle birds flying east and flock of ducks flying way over old camp and I took two picture of camp and didn't work the camra right that was too bad. I was over to traps. Nothing.

**May 27<sup>th</sup>.** · I was over to little islands and I saw two sea gulls flying and I saw flock of geese and two doidle birds flying and I sav another flock of geese this morning and I saw fox tracks over little Island. And I made myself a sun bonnert and I got some roots tea tin half full. Today I was going over to old camp but it was too windy and has been drifting last night in to storm shade.

**May 28<sup>th</sup>.** I over to the old camp and see if there is any birds a round but there is nothing it looks more winter then over here. And when I was on my way down I saw one fox way out on the ice going south west. And when I come home I chop wood and clean fox skins three of them and put them strechers.

**May 29<sup>th</sup>.** I didn't do nothing today. Oh but I was feel tired from that long walk I had to old camp. And I saw spider on sand today and I took cadarpillar from old camp. I didn't see nothing today.

**May 30.** I was feel pretty sick this morning but this afternoon I feel better I saw five flocks of geese today and hear doedle bird some where but I didn't see it.

**May' 31<sup>st</sup>.** I didn't get few sticks of wood. And I site two places of traps for see gull and I hear geese but didn't see them and I open case of biscuits.

**June 1st**. I didn't do nothing today becuase I was not feel ling well I saw doedle bird over end of sand spit.

**June 2nd**. I seat up the tent today and I out hunding birds over the Island and I saw flock of brand way over in land and I saw two pin tail birds and I got one flie from the Islands.

**June 3rd**. I didn't go no where today just cleaning two {'ox skins and I saw two flocks of geese and one raven I hear another flock of geese but I didn't see them.

**June 4th**. I clean one good fox skin and two are füll of she Is ( ? ) that cat has been trying eat the fox skin that Galle got and I saw banch of smale see galles and one mach smeler. And I saw duck flying over the ice and brand four of them flying over camp very high and I clean shotgun and rifle and I made smele little picke for roots.

**June 5**. I didn't do nothing today but reading Bible I just finish old testaments the next I will read new testaments. And snowing al day.

**June 6th**. I was over to the Island and got some sweet roots I shot one doedle bird I saw only two and I saw a Polar bear it was way out on the ice first I saw him and from south of camp he turn tourch camp and to just got about on the beach he went out to south again and then/west and went to the beach and it went out south again last I saw it and it got snowing and I cann't see him again. knight said he was fianting last night he is just dieing he could hardly talk. I shot three times today and got only with one.

**June 7th**. I going over to the Island get some sweet roots and when I got close to the end of the Island (?) the see gall and I took a shot at him and I got him dead shot. Oh my! it good and I eat no meat for long time and I saw two shadhurk (?) and I made smale little picke and I made rifle resting board so its handy if I seal hund when I t m ready to so I don t t have to look a place to rest my rifle.

**June 8<sup>th</sup>**. I was over the and got some roots and I saw three doedle birds I took a shot at one doedle bird didn't get him and when I come home there two Idare ducks flying and got shotgun in my hands got the hammer ready and there were too far and I forgot the hammer was ready and I pull the tricker boom it went didn't hurt me. And I made shotgun cartridge bag and I shide pan for Imight he try to put the pan under him. He just bearly make it, I had to cut it open space on his sleeping bag sp he can put the pan. And I can see tracks on the beach with the field glasses I think they are polar bear tracks one looks fresh and one looks old.

**June 9<sup>th</sup>**. I was over to west end of the over there but didn't get see gall and I found one when I was coming home there was geese fly over me geese and she had three eggs in her one almost got shot at shid    but didn't kill her and I saw harbard I was boombarting fresh see gall Egg and and I took a shot I got one shell on it and I took a little sumrner bird.

(Second part of Ada Blackjack's diary, written in a book of order blanks for photographic supplies.)

June 10, 1923.

writtin by Mrs. Ada B. Jack

Wrangel Island

**Mr. knight told me to use this, diary**

**June 10.** This very important noted in case I happen to got died or some body fine out and found that I was dead I want she Mrs. Rita McCafferty take care of my son Bennett. I don't want has his father Black Jack to take him on a count of stepmother not one for my boy. My sister Rita is just as good his on mother I know egg she love Bennett just as much as I do I dare not my son to have and stepmother. If you please let this how to the Judge. If I got any two money coming from boss of this company if $1, 200.00 give my smale my mother Mrs. Ototook $200.00 if its only $600.00 give her ones $100.00 rest of it for my son. And let Rita have money enough meat. to support Bennett.

Mrs. Ada B. Jack,

I just write noted in cage Polar bear tear me down or case I fall in some (?) in ice becuase I am hunding pretty near every day knight is very sick he hardly talk and he is skiny my he nothing but skin and bone he lay in his sleeping bag for four month he pretty near die 10th of May and 12th. I t m hunding with shotgun every day pretty near I got one doedle bird and next (?) ix got see gall and then one geese I shot geese when they fly over me and today I cann't go out hunding on a count my eyes sore from snow blind today is June 10th yesterday I got geese and I found one see gall egg and that one geese I knight eat some egg he cann i t eat

**June 10th.** I cann t t go snow blind and rain.

97

**June 11<sup>th</sup>**. I didn't go no where today on acount of my eyes sore from snow blind I just getting wood and clean shotgun that one that I don't use.

**June 12<sup>th</sup>**. I didn't go out nowhere today on account of my eyes on boam.

**June 13<sup>th</sup>**. I went to the end of the harbar and I found nine see gall eggs today and I got one see gall and I wash the dishes. I took two shots with the rifle trying to get see gall didn't hide them and I saw three brand fly by me too far to shot with shotgun and I saw flock of geese.

**June 14<sup>th</sup>**. I didn't go no where today just getting wood and I stard to Imit gloves for myself few Idars fly a round.

**June 15<sup>th</sup>**. I just knitting gloves for myself and today I hear loan.

**June 16.** I finish my knit gloves and I got see gall in the trap.

**June 17.** I wash my clothes today and i shot once to a Idars. and this evening I made a target and shot two times with the rifle. and I took my target in and show it to knight and he said its pretty good shooting and I saw a creek flowing to the harbar.

**June 18.** I was out seal hunding this evening from five till eleven and I do some target shooting today I shot three times standing up I only hit the target once oh yes I shot at seal twice didn't hit it and I saw another seal right by it I thought it was same seal I fine it wasn't.

**June 19.** I stay home today having rest and this evening I get one female Idar I was after two brand but they flow before I got there.

**June 20.** I was out to the west to get some eggs but there is no way to go to eggs water all around they are on smale sand

Island see gall out hunding today my eyes is sore from eggs that
I found I made little sack with the rifle I didn't meant to but it
want set, knight is getting very bad he looks like he is going to
die.

**June 22nd**. I move to the other tent today and I was my
dishes and getting some wood.

**June 23d**. I out to the old camp today and got some sweet
roots and shot two Black and white wing birds and I was going
to the camp but I cann't crose the river I just, gets some roots

**June 24**. I was out ducking today and I got four Idars two
Tamale and two male of Idar ducks one I lost it when I shot her
so she cann t t fly she dieve and I didn't know where it went and
I took pictures of this tent and myself I don't know how I work
the camra.

**June 25**. I was over other side of harbar mouth and I got
seven eidars three male and four female. and when I came home
I pluck them and cut them hunge the breast and the legs to dry.

**June 26**. I was taking walk over to little Island and I found
three see gall eggs in one nest. and I cook them for my lunch I
take tea and saccharine I had a nice piclmick all by myself.

**June 27**. I was after a seal right out in the front of the camp
she went dovm on me they were two o? them in one place and I
came back and took myself a picture try anyway and I went to
the east and I saw a seal and I went aftér it and got it with one
shot they were two but the other went down and I got the other.
That t s a frist seal I ever got in my life.

**June 28th**. I stay at home today and clean seal skin and let
this afternoon I hear some ihnny noise so I look out thought the
door and saw polar bear and one cub. I was very afriad so I took
a shot over them see if they would go so they went away and

99

June
21
.
I
was
tryin
g to
them
and I
carr
y
rifle
so I
can
shot
for
Idar
dow
ns.
g
e
t
I
d
a
r
d
uck but I
cann t t
get, close
to but I
cann i t
get any
chance
and I
boam

they were looking back and I shot five times and they run away. I thQ-;k God that is true living God.

**June 29<sup>th</sup>**. I am home all day becuase I got monthly and I fix my bed and I went after a seal she was up between from end of the sand spit and I shot two times before she went down and when I carne back after trying to get that seal I fieal the back sight and shot target and I hit where I amiam and I shot old milk can pretty near hit it I think the sight of rifle is better now.

**June 60**. I made seal skin strecher and put the seal to day. and mended my yarn gloves.

**July 1<sup>st</sup>**. I stay home touy and I fix the shovel handle that I brack this spring and I saw polar bear out cn the ice and this evening I went to the end of the sand spit shot a eidar duck I shot him right in the head thank God keep me a live till now.

**July 2<sup>nd</sup>**. I put up four Poles and put real s so I can go on top of them and look a round with the field glasses and this evening I was my head. July 3d. I stay at home today and read I read about smiaratan Woman she was talking to Jusses.

**July 4<sup>th</sup>**. I was after a seal that was on the mouth of the harbar they were two and one on front of camp so they went down on me those two seals so I went aftér the one that was right front of camp and I got the rifle already and wait for him to put his head up and rifle was already hammer was ready so I look some thing and move around boan it went and the seal went down and I stand up and say fourth of July. I was surpprised rifle boan so I had my fourth of July.it was not rian this morning and this afternoon its rain.

**July 5**. I after three seals right on mouth of the harbor I shoot twice but I got only one and I cone home and cut up the seal and hange the meat tb dry and put the skin on the stretcher to day all done at one day and this evening I took a bath. I thank the lord Je sus .

**July 6.** I was after seal over the harbar mouth and one on front of camp and I shot it second time I after it and when I got I went back and get pulling line and when I was close to the seal 1 saw bear out on the ice running tourch east and I ran back and they were dragging seal I took a shot over them becuase they were too far and they went west and then they went on the beach and came east and pass the camp over other siad of harbar mouth and it got very fogy and this evening it got clear and I saw that they ate the seal I shot. and I saw them not very far on the ice and I took one shot and they went west. and I cut a pair of sole for my boats and this afternoon I open box of shotgun cartridges.

**July 7<sup>th</sup>.** I was try to get a duck but didn't have any chance to shot and I sgrup the skin soles for my boat and this afternoon Polar bear and young one was to the seal again I think they are same bears that I saw yester— day and they were right little east of the camp and I try to shot them but I didn't hit them. and I fix the tent door put new piece on it,

**July 8.** I was trying to get a duck with rifle I finely shot one but I could not get on a count of raton ice on the harbor mouth female eidar duck and this afternoon I chew up my boat soles and this evening I put the dried meat in the box and the box is full.

**July 9.** I took a shot at old sqaw and I shot two but 1 could not get them they are on the water round in raiton ice in the harbor end. and I took two three shoots to the target I only hit once and I put new soles on my boats today and got one more pair ready for my short boats. and I put piece of canves on the tent Tram.

**July 10.** I stay home all day very nice and sünshines. I t m glad to have a nice rest today.

**July 11.** I put new soles on my short boats very nice day today. I thank the heavenly father for today oh yes I open new can of tea.

**July 12.** I knit the fingers of Muaras gloves and this afternoon I do some fancy sewing o? about one and half foot I made for a parky.

**July IS.** I sewed a fancy skin for parky and I made about half a crose the parky boodem.

**July 14.** I sew fancy dkin today and only 11 more it will be all ready to put around the parky I should say 11 pieces very nice day.

**July 15.** I finished the fancy skin for my parky trimming.

**July 16.** I was out hunding this morning and I got two gray birds smele ones and this afternoon I made a canves boat it works all right this afternoon I got three old sqaws and I use the boat I made.

**July 17.** I had a good rest today. thank God.

**July 18.** I got two old sqews this morning and afternoon I shot one eidar duck with the rifle and I fell the box with dried seal meat and I took out the seal skins from the stretcher and this morning I made one patte for my canves boat.

**July 19.** I sqrieped one raindeer skin for my parky and I sew the hook and made wolf trirming. this evening around the beach got open water and another open laid of about half a mile from the sore.

**July 20.** I nearly finished my parky today just around the hood and around sleeve and the fancy trimming oh yes I sqriep the skin frist and then I start to sew. and this morning when I got up I saw new pile of ice over west side of harbar mouth.

July 21st. I put fancy trimming on my new parky and trimming around the hood, it look like a parky alright. and my new park-y is all finished today.

July 22st. I made two patte today for my canves boat and I got two old sqews today.

July 23. I made my inside parky smaler on the side and fix the wolf triming and put another piece of fancy skin on the boodem rain this morning and wind blowing hard from east. and I saw bear and two young ones there are near east end of the harbar on inland side. I thank God for living. July 24. I stay home today and read. and I hear walrus I 've been hearing them for about two or three days .

July 25. I load up brass shells this afternoon and then I went out hunt I got two old sqevs today. very nice day.

July 26. I made sort boats of raindeer skin and slepers I sqrieped the legens last night. and I got one little gray bird and I took the moldy biscits to the other box and clean ones to the box oh yes I dreamed last night I was singing three cheer for the red white and blue.

July 27. I made fancy tops for my deer legen sort boats and put piece of red skin around and on the slepers I got my sort boats already put soles.

July 28. I sqrieped skin for my boats soles and soak it. and I open box of shotgun cartridges and then got one old sqaw. and I clean seal flapers and put them away in case ship comes so I can take them home and eat them with my sisters if the lord let me have it thank.

**July 29.** I put soles on my fancy short boats and got the soles ready for slepers. this evening I found two of gray birds eggs about two or three hundred yards from my tent .

**July 30.** I put soles on my new raindeer legens s lepers and this afternoon I took a bath and when I got thought bathing I took the water out and I took a walk to the beach and look with the glasses and I saw Polar bear and two young ones and when I came back to the tent I saw another one over east of the Camp bear and and the ice is broken to piece

**July 31st.** I thank the young ones are over north west inland. quite many open leads . living God thought Jusses that keeped me alive till now. how much more I thank Jusses that forgives the sinners and theen to help them blessed is he of whom the savour of sinners.

**Aug. 1st.** I was bunch of my durdy clothes and this afternoon I sew bead on to Bennetts slepers if I should got home so he can put slepers on. and this late afternoon I walk over to the end of the spit and I saw bear tracks fresh. very nice today thank 1 iving God thought Juses that help me every day and night if God be with me till I should get home again I thank God very much that he had mercy on me and foregive my sins.

**Aug. 2.** I was hunting this morning and got one old sqaw and three smale gray birds I start to salt birds now oh yes I found one smale gray bird young one over other side and I forgot the canves boat to hold up and it has been drift away and I made another canves boat better one this time I didn't finish it I t 11 finishe it the morrow if God permitt me.

**Aug. 3.** I finished new canves boat and it is only thing this time and I went over other side of the harbar mouth and got some green and I boil them when I come home and I saw flock of brand over the little Island and latter I saw bear he went inland

I guess the ice is going out its very much open around the beach oh yes I made oars for my new boat. I thank God.

**Aug. 4.** I finished Bennetts slepers today oh they are qured looking things it look like ice is out I cannt see very far its very fogy but both ways out from beach it look clear the ice cakes don't drifting in around ruche and today L found bear track east side of the tent thank living God is love.

**Aug.** I was out once surely the ice this evening I thank God. **5.** I was just reading to about Frederick A. Cook. and with my canves boat try to get some old sqaw but no chance.

is going out it moving to the west quite many open sea and saw bear and young one just one way inland going torch inland.

**August. 6.** I got one gray little bird that had two eggs east side of camp and I took the eggs when I got the bird and I saw flock of geese inland flying east fogy all day can not see very far and I wash my hair today. thank the lord Jesus Christ the saviour.

**Aug. 7.** I was home today reading Frederick A. Cook this morning was clear and fogy this afternoon and early evening get clear and sun begin to sets I open one tooth dental cream the ice on the ocean is almost out of s ight.

**Aug. 8.** Now I see the ocean is pretty clear so it looks like it I was going to see boat coming pretty fogy today but some times I can see a mile or two and I made waist sort of croaset. I thank saviour Jesus that keep me from loneliness.

**Aug. 9.** I made new fur inside o? my moose mittens and I put loges over the tent and fixing around tent today and late in afternoon I got one old sqaw.

**Aug. 16.** I try to got old sqaw but no chance I hit one and eider duck but didn't hit them. I saw bunch of walrus little south east of camp and I saw ograk right back of the tent close to the sore and I saw it again mouth of harbar.

**Aug. 11.** I haul wood from other side I found young brid so I took to the camp and take pictures of her I took pictures of a whole film and I put another film and took one more just put her on top of box. and I knit seal net so I can use it soon. thank the lord Jesus.

**Aug. 12.** I just knit seal net today this morning when I got up I found lard can was empty that was full seal blubber the Polar bear has been eating last night. I thank the lord Jesus keep me from danger. the wind is from west first time for about whole monthe and I dreamed night before that the boss ask me if would have things creited from the store
I said it will be case or nothing fore being stay here for two years

**Aug. 13.** I finished the seal net ready to put robe and I unravel the new sock and start to knit gloves for myself. I thank the savour Jesus.

**Aug. 14.** I took pictures of myself and the bird that I shot and I took pictures of mountains. I thank the savour Jesus.

**Aug. 15.** I was knitting today. and this evening I saw bunch of walrus out front Camp of about one mile off sore big bunch of them. I thank the savour Jesus Christ.

**Aug. 16.** I got two little birds today and I saw bunch of walrus front Camp about one mile I think they are the same bunch that I saw last night. i made a elder duck skin cap Cdr Ma.

**Aug. 17.** I took a shot at walrus that flooding on top of the ice I hit him alright but on the body. I thank God throught savour Jesus Christ. and I thank esus loves my little boy Bennett.

**Aug. 18**. I finish right of my glove and I unravel the another sock and stard the other side. I thank God.

**Aug. 19.** the wind blowing hard frome west and the ice is going out slowly few days ago I though it was going out but didn't go very far. I saw eider duck and four young ones back of the tent. I thank God through Jesus our savour.

**Aug. 20.** I finished my knited gloves today and I open last biscuit box. the ice is over little below horizon. I thank the lord Jesus and his father.

# PART THREE

———————

EPILOGUE

## TRIP TO RAUNER COLLECTIONS
## AT DARTMOUTH

—————

February 27, 2018, I gave a reading at Brown University in Providence, Rhode Island where I had driven from Kansas. The next day, I drove on a snowy highway 182 miles north to Hanover, New Hampshire, to visit the Rauner Collections in Dartmouth's Library in Webster Hall where Ada Blackjack's diary and papers are housed.

Afterwards I returned to Kansas. 1,400 miles in two days. Before a Nor-easter hit and continued with two more storms following. I was on the east coast in an opening between storms.

I like the contingencies. The off-chutes off-shooting.
There are unrealized parts within the realized. I find places of it like driftwood on the shore of Wrangel Island. This exploration of the life of Ada Blackjack, educated and evangelized in a Methodist Mission.

Driftwood became a metaphor for Ada's singular expedition into self-reliance and survival.

The shore of Wrangel Island was cluttered with driftwood. Spruce, larch, fir and pine from timber rafting in Siberia and North America. Some of the wood set adrift if for some reason was useless for building. Sometimes the wood was caught in the ice long enough to be transformed into unearthly shapes.

The driftwood became an archetype of faith as Ada remembered her belief in Christ when she was alone on the island. Jesus drifted from Ada's lessons at the Methodist Mission into her writing. The idea of the cross also is a type of driftwood.

Aug. 6.  thank the lord Jesus Christ the saviour

Aug. 8.  I thank saviour Jesus that keep me from loneliness.

Aug. 11. thank the Lord Jesus

Aug. 13  I thank the  savour Jesus

Aug. 14  I thank the savour Jesus

Aug. 15  I thank the savour Jesus Christ

Aug. 18  I thank God

Aug. 19  I thank God through Jesus our savour

Three days before her rescue she wrote—

Aug 20. I finished my knitted gloves today and I open last biscuit box. the ice is over little below horizon. I thank the lord Jesus and his father.

# TRIP TO ALASKA

June 12-13, 2018, I was in Homer, Alaska, for the Kachemak Bay Writer's Conference.

It was an easy flight. 3½ hours from Kansas City to Seattle. 3½ hours from Seattle to Anchorage. 45 minutes from Anchorage to Homer. I had a 6:00 a.m. flight from Kansas. I arrived in Homer around 4 in the afternoon with a 4-hour difference in time. With layovers— probably 14 hours start to finish.

During flight, I watched the long streaks of clouds like waves coming into shore.

I have a piece of driftwood on my bookcase in Kansas that looks like a fish. I found it on the Lake of the Ozarks in Missouri when I was in college at the University of Missouri.

Walking on the shore at Kachemak Bay in Alaska, I found a small piece of driftwood, much like a finger, only longer. I put it in my roller bag.

The ravens followed me there.

I felt the struggle for survival. The necessity to hunt. To eat. To observe the minute happenings across the ice that was the work of Ada's inner journey. The imaginative journal I felt beneath the words she wrote in her diary. The part of herself buried in tracings over fragments of her writing that led to thought behind the entries. It's the translation of the English I distilled into English.

"I read the Old Testament. Now the New"— she wrote— as if that was a simple task.

I wanted to know Ada's thoughts on being literate. On learning penmanship. The meaning of it. Making marks for letters. The discovery that literacy was more than writing. More than meat and potatoes, though there were no potatoes there. They were rotten on arrival at Wrangel Island. I realized Ada's developing consciousness of self and identity of difference from others. It is between the sentences she wrote. There was an individualization of Ada Blackjack that she did not yet put into words. But there it is in the crevices. It is in her diary. It is in the calendar book on which she marked off her days.

Vilhjalmur Stefansson, Arctic explorer and ethnologist, purchased the diary for $500. It remains in the Rauner Collections at Dartmouth College. Ada's diary is mundane. But beneath it is her story, like the roots she dug for beneath the snow on Wrangel Island.

I had images of a tea pot, needle, thimble, sinew. Sacraments of boredom. Arctic hysteria— a fight against isolation, overwhelming hardship, danger, and the uncertainty of survival. The outlier experience Ada suffered on Wrangel Island.

I could imagine Ada Blackjack walking on the gravel shore of the island when all the world was alone.

She wrote what she did each day. "I didn't do nothing today," she wrote once.

No. Nothing was not something she did.

Ada could sew. She could cook. She could speak English. She was alone. She was poor. She was useful. Useable. She could provide what the men needed on their mission to claim Wrangel Island.

I also found Ada useful for exploration. An Inupiat who did not learn Inupiat ways of survival because she was in a mission boarding school. Yet in the Arctic, she had to act on what she didn't know. She had to create the means of survival from erasure. I wanted to go over and over her story. I've always liked peripheral journeys. I've liked the bridges that faith provides. I wanted to see Ada by the ocean under the Arctic sky, wandering with stars.

# APPENDIX

---

## *VENTRILOQUATE*
Or, Ventriloquism and a Treatise on Giving Voice

———————

WRITING IS AN ACT of ventriloquism. Giving voice to another— a ventriloquistic act. Someone doesn't have a voice. Mute in history. Silent in research libraries. Left on the shelf. No one keeping record of their words. Or if words were kept, not the tone in which they were meant. The voice of the land also calling to be heard. A residue of land. I've known for years. Have heard when I traveled to their places. The voice of the land there to be listened. The animals, also. The voiceless speak to me without moving their mouth. It is a texture of silence. To speak without one's mouth moving. I speak for them also without moving mine.

Ventriloquist, from the Latin venter [belly] and loqui [speak].

Ventriloquism, as from the belly. The engine room rumbling there. To be the one that speaks a voice that seems to come from somewhere else in the vast mystery.

Was it them giving voice to me? Or me to them? Or was it us finding voices within Voice?

Originally a religious practice [Wikipedia]. The noises from the stomach were thought to be from the dead.

Ventriloquism is of ancient origin. Traces found in Egypt in Hebrew archaeology. Eurycles of Athens. Many adept in ventriloquism— the Eskimos [Wikipedia again].

Throwing voice to another. Speaking for another who cannot speak on their own. From my own stomach. The growling of the ancestors from the hunger that haunts. Late in the evening. I hear them.

Now cannibalistic tendencies buried there. As happened on expeditions in the cold in hunger and dread of death and no survivors to tell the story that later a ventriloquist could handle. What happened to those men? Did you eat them? No. I only spoke for them disappearing as they did on the way to Siberia for help.

Writing is an act of ventriloquism. Writing does not move its mouth unless reading [later] what is written. And even then, there is disconnect from the stomach of the written word from the voice that speaks it.

All the fraudulence that writing takes to write. To say in the voice of another. As they stand there mute in history. Putting voices into their mouth. Swallowing thoughts inside their heads.

The dark gray gravel on the shore of Alaska. The rough barrenness. The driftwood on the shore in long sentences.

Speaking without my mouth— moving from the belly. The inner place that only can be reached by swallowing.

The Hunger of the Polar Bear [in a ventriloquistic act]—

I am hungry. I am hungry. My stomach growls. Hunger is an iceberg. Hunger is the sky. Hunger is the sun on snow. I want. I want. Hunger growls like the motor of the boat that brought them to the island. Hunger is vast. It is a strong wind that blows my fur backwards. Hunger burns my eyes. Tightens my jaw. My mouth waters. I chew as if I am eating. I wait at the airhole for a seal. I wait. I wait. The edge crumbles into the sea. I fall in the water. I crawl back onto the ice. I think of the seal in my mouth. I chew. I chew. Nothing is there. Seal blood once stained my face red as the sun when it starts to rise.

And the voice of the driftwood— stories of where it came from. The pieces are only parts of what they had been. They left their roots to travel in the ocean. [Fallen trees carried by the rivers. From rivers they went into the ocean. Caught in northward currents. They arrive in the Arctic.] My words are lines of driftwood. They arrive from someplace else. I sit beside the driftwood on the shore. I hold it like a river.

## A STORY WITHIN A STORY

---

The stage lighting was no doubt avant-garde for that period: the curtains simulating the Northern Lights, constantly dispatched mysterious waves of light in our direction—
    Yoko Tawada, *Memoirs of a Polar Bear*

A DREAM IS A SCAR LINE. Something unresolved. Or, if resolved, a rise in the skin remains. A mark. Sparse lines of text as if sled tracks through the snow.

Ada's fear of the polar bear interrupting.

I thought of what to do. How to splice the Arctic voices together.

The Arctic as the edge of a stage on which fragments of dialogue were heard—

Polar Bear
It was the polar bear who made the world.
The ice.
The glaciers.

Ptarmigan
It was the ptarmigan who made the polar bear.

Polar Bear
I came from the green and blue tunnels of the Northern Lights.

Ptarmigan
You are not alone here— Arctic fox, wolverine, Arctic wolf, Arctic hare, penguin, seal, walrus, whale, snowy owl, Arctic tern, puffin, moose, caribou, white ermine. The Arctic is an animal herd.

Polar Bear
I wait at the breathing hole for a seal.
I sing the seal a song— *Uh—Uh—Uh—Uh—*

The little ptarmigan struts in the snow. Brown in summer. White in winter. With foot feathers and pectinations— those bristly projections that make him the little Big Foot of the Arctic.

Ptarmigan
Strut. Strut.

Polar Bear
He eats seeds, buds, berries, twigs, leaves and any vegetation he can find in the snow.

Ptarmigan
Peck. Peck.

Polar Bear
He lays spotted eggs in his little snow den.

Sometimes I eye him. He's not big enough for a meal.
I want ringed seal. Bearded seal. Walrus. Beluga whale. Bowhead whale.
Meanwhile, I lick oil cans behind the explorers' tent.
I dream a seal drops off the moon— the high diving board— into the sea.
It swims and then surfaces at the air hole. I claw it, lifting it to my mouth.

Ptarmigan
I see the shadow of the snow owl flying on the ice. It circles in its mystery— its waves of light.

# POSTSCRIPT

---

WHAT IS TRUE, AFTER ALL? Two voices whose lives did not overlap. Who spoke in tandem, nonetheless. The second voice haunted by the first. Or the second voice wrapped around the first voice in an act of cannibalism. Or the second voice as little embroideries that surround the first voice. Distinct in different places, different times, yet working as if time and place did not matter, as a line of driftwood from various places gathered on the shore. I am not alone, Ada kept saying. Repetition itself a thread following the needle.

Stranded. Interrupted by a polar story. On an island by oneself. Wounded and in the wounding bearing the scar that becomes an island in the memory of the journey's loss—
Allan Crawford, Lorne Knight, Fred Maurer, Milton Galle.

## ACKNOWLEDGMENTS

————————

*Michigan Quarterly Review, Why We Write* issue edited by Mark Nowak, for "Ventriloquate," under the title, "Ventriloquism and a Treatise on Writing [mainly historical] which I often do."

The Kachemak Bay Writer's Conference, Homer, Alaska, for a first reading of *A Line of Driftwood* during faculty readings. Thanks to Carol Swartz and Peggy Shumaker for the invitation to participate. Thanks, also, to Barbara Hurd.

The Rauner Collection, Dartmouth College, for Ada Blackjack's diary from which extrapolations were taken. Thanks especially to Laura Schieb, reference specialist.

Sarah dAngelo, Drama Department, Brown University for the invitation to read.

Jennifer Nivens, *Ada Blackjack, a True Story of Survival in the Arctic*, Hachette Books, 2003.

Ruth Greenstein and Turtle Point Press for publication.

And lastly, for the isolation of Covid that brought Ada's isolation home.

*ABOUT THE AUTHOR*

Diane Glancy is a poet, novelist, essayist, playwright, and professor emeritus at Macalester College. Her works have won the Pablo Neruda Prize for Poetry, the Arrell Gibson Lifetime Achievement Award from the Oklahoma Center for the Book, the Lifetime Achievement Award from the Native Writers' Circle of the Americas, and more. In 2018, *Publishers Weekly* named her book *Pushing the Bear: A Novel of the Trail of Tears* one of the ten essential Native American novels. Glancy divides her time between Kansas and Texas.